136322

THIS WALKER BOOK BELONGS TO:

_____

_____

_____

_____

For Barnaby

The Check-up and
The Birthday Party first published 1983
Our Dog first published 1984
by Walker Books Ltd
87 Vauxhall Walk
London SE11 5HJ

This edition published 1995

2 4 6 8 10 9 7 5 3 1

© 1983, 1984 Helen Oxenbury

This book has been typeset in Goudy.

Printed in Hong Kong

British Library Cataloguing in Publication Data
A catalogue record for this book is available from the British Library.

ISBN 0-7445-3777-0 (hb)
ISBN 0-7445-3722-3 (pb)

One Day with Mum

Helen Oxenbury

WALKER BOOKS
AND SUBSIDIARIES
LONDON · BOSTON · SYDNEY

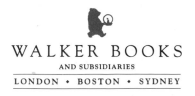

Our Dog

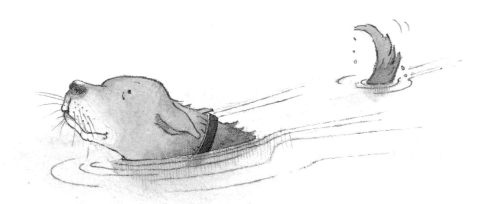

Our dog has to go for a walk
every day.
She stares at us until we
take her.

One day she found a smelly pond
and jumped into it.
"Poo! You smell disgusting!"
we told her.

Then she rolled in the mud.
"Pretend she's not ours,"
whispered Mum. "We must get her
home quickly and give her a bath."

We made her wait outside
the kitchen door.
Mum filled the bath.
"I'll put her in," Mum said.
"Now hold on tight!
Don't let her jump out!"

"Quick! Where's the towel?"
Mum shouted. "She'll make
everything wet!"

We chased her out
of the kitchen

and down the hall.
She ran up the
stairs and into
the bedroom.

18

We caught her on the bed.
"It's no good!" Mum said.
"We'll just have to take her for
another walk, to dry in the air."

The Check-up

Mum took me to the doctor
for a check-up.
"You'll have to wait your turn,"
the nurse said.
The waiting room smelt funny.
I opened the window.

Nobody wanted to talk to me.
"Perhaps they're not feeling
well," Mum whispered.

"Who's next?" the doctor said.

"Come on, it's our turn," Mum said.

"I want to go home," I said.

"Well, young man, shall we have
a listen to your chest?"
I sat on Mum's lap.
"Look," Mum said. "It doesn't hurt."

"If you do what the doctor says,"
Mum whispered, "I'll buy you
a little something on the way home."

"Let's go home now, Mum," I said.
The doctor fell off his chair.

31

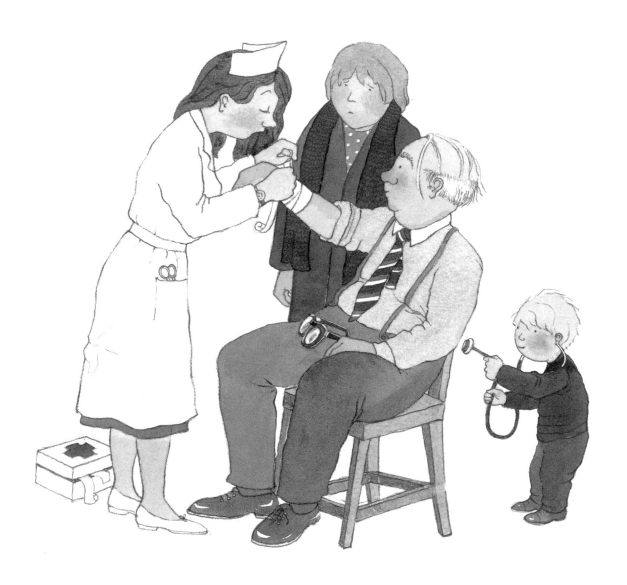

"Call the nurse," said the doctor.
"I'm so sorry," said Mum.

"He seems normal enough,"
the doctor said. "I won't
need to see him again
for some time, I hope."
"I like the doctor," I said.
"I think he's really nice."

The Birthday Party

36

I chose John's birthday
present on my own. "Can't
I try them out, Mum?"
"No," Mum said, "we
bought them for John."

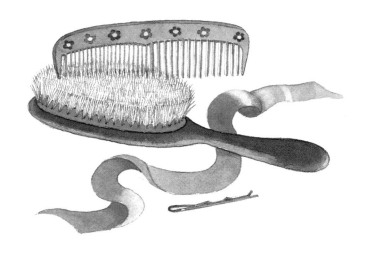

"Let's have your blue
ribbon as well," Mum said.

"Is that my present?"
John said when we arrived.

"Happy birthday, John," Mum said.
She made me give him the present.

"Here's my cake," John shouted.
He just left my present on the floor.
After tea we had games and
balloons and running about
and jumping and bumping.

My dad collected me.
"Give her the balloon,"
John's mum said.
"Do you really want it?"
John said.
"Yes please," I said. "I do."

MORE WALKER PAPERBACKS
For You to Enjoy

Growing up with Helen Oxenbury

TOM AND PIPPO

There are six stories in each of these two colourful books about
toddler Tom and his special friend Pippo, a soft-toy monkey.

"Just right for small children… A most welcome addition to the nursery shelves." *Books for Keeps*

At Home with Tom and Pippo   0-7445-3721-5
Out and About with Tom and Pippo   0-7445-3720-7
£3.99 each

THREE PICTURE STORIES

Each of the titles in this series contains three classic stories of pre-school life,
first published individually as First Picture Books.

"Everyday stories of family life, any one of these humorous depictions of
the trials of an under five will be readily identified by children and adults …
buy them all if you can." *Books For Your Children*

One Day with Mum   0-7445-3722-3
A Bit of Dancing   0-7445-3723-1
A Really Great Time   0-7445-3724-X
£3.99 each

MINI MIX AND MATCH BOOKS

Originally published as Heads, Bodies and Legs these fun-packed
little novelty books each contain 729 possible combinations!

"Good value, highly imaginative, definitely to be looked out for." *Books For Your Children*

Animal Allsorts   0-7445-3705-3
Puzzle People   0-7445-3706-1
£2.99 each